BLUE EAGLE
meets
Double Trouble

Written by:
Steven E. Jones

Illustrated by:
Steven E. Jones, Jr.

Blue Eagle Meets Double Trouble

Copyright©2008 by Blue Eagle Books, Inc.

Cover Design by Steven E. Jones, Jr.

Printed and bound in China by Leo Paper

ISBN-13: 978-0-9794655-0-5
ISBN-10: 0-9794655-0-8

BLUE
EAGLE
BOOKS

5773 Woodway Dr.
PMB 190
Houston, TX 77057

Tel: (713) 789-1516
www.blueeaglebooks.com

DEDICATION

This book is dedicated to all the descendants and friends of
my father who were privileged to have heard him tell his
"Blue Eagle" stories. I specifically want to thank my
brother and sister-in-law, Harry R. Jones, Jr. and Elouise,
for consistently encouraging us to continue this series.
They have reached the pinnacle of Blue Eagle's helpers!

Steven E. Jones

Chapter 1

North of Peaceful Valley it started to rain.
It continued so long, the land couldn't drain.

Now Blue Eagle's brother lived in that land
And he sent word to Blue to come give him a hand.

So Blue told his friends he'd be gone for a while,
But if they'd work together it should not be a trial.

Then off he flew to the North in a hurry,
Saying, "Help one another and try not to worry!"

But not too long after Blue had departed,
Came reason to worry about being unguarded!

Coming down from the North, chased by the rains
Were two hungry coyotes with a shortage of brains!

Driven by hunger to the Valley they trod,
Expecting a feast, these two - Clem and Clod!

Coyotes have a way of announcing everything,
You know where they are
'cause they think they can sing!

They barked and they yapped
and they howled at the moon;
To the critters below it was some awful tune!

"Yip, yip, yip and a howl, yes, a howl,
Two cagey coyotes out on the prowl.
Whenever you hear us start to sing,
It means we're ready to do our thing.
Gonna catch us a rabbit or a squirrel
And put the whole valley in a whirl!
We coyotes hunt by sight and by smell,
So we can sniff out wherever you dwell.
Don't try to hide with chances this slim,
'Cause we are the brothers, Clod and Clem!
Yip, yip, yip and a howl, yes, a howl,
Two cagey coyotes out on the prowl."

Down in the Valley, Pete Rabbit gathered the gang.
"I heard them," he said, "and got chills when they sang!
The coyotes are coming and I know what they seek,
Remember the lessons from our game 'Sneak and Peek'!
Those who can fly should most certainly flee
And those who can climb should get up in a tree."

"Swimmers to the river - stay away from the sides,
And everyone else go wherever he hides!
When hiding, be sure that you stay concealed
And don't move at all until safety is revealed.
Those coyotes are dastardly, loud and uncouth;
They're out to get us and we know that's the truth!"

After Pete had explained the frightful situation,
Everyone moved toward their own safety station.

Owl, Duck, and Jaybird took to the air;
Sammy, Rio, and Chip found a tree to share.

Toby the Turtle left with Arny and Laverne,
The coyotes' dinner was his big concern.

"The three of us have natural protection;
Together perhaps we can change their direction."

Chapter 2

Into the valley came the brothers, Clem and Clod.
Silence and calm - they thought it quite odd.

Clem said to Clod, "This valley's too still.
We should see critters, our stomachs to fill."

They looked high and low and sniffed at the air.
Finally, Clod said, "What's that, over there?

See those two rocks over by the flowers?
One of them moved, now it will be ours!"

Clod moved in to check out this fellow,
Said, "That's not a rock; it's an armadillo.

The other one looks to be just a turtle.
Come on Clem, they won't be a hurdle."

Then Arny took off - for the flowers he scurried,
Clem gave chase, but Clod wasn't worried.

Arny passed Laverne as she raised herself up;
Clem yelped, then whined like a scared little pup.

"Help me Clod, help me! I'm blind and I'm sick!
I've run into a skunk who unloaded her trick!"

Clod rose to see what caused Clem to fail,
And suddenly barked, "What has hold of my tail?"

It was Toby and he was holding on tight.
Now these coyotes had become quite a sight!

Clod cried, "I'm gonna run 'til he lets go,
I'll come back to help as soon as it's so."

To the river he hurried, giving Toby a dunk,
But the water's his home; its fun to 'kerplunk'!

Clod fled from the river, dragging Toby by his teeth,
Through painted meadows and weeds, seeking relief.

Spring in the valley brings colors galore;
Lush grasses, wild flowers, and oh so much more!

Into these fields Clod charged with a rush,
Through bluebonnets, sage, and scarlet paintbrush.

Up to the hilltop, through thicket and hollow;
Wherever he went, Toby would follow!

The rest of the day, although he was worn,
Clod kept dragging Toby 'til it all seemed forlorn.

All of this time
Clem wandered and fell,
His eyes were a blur
and his nose wouldn't smell!

About this time he felt
a tug on his back,
And was lifted up high
to the sound of a quack.

Blue had been retrieved
by old Daniel Duck
And he said to Clem,
"You've run out of luck!"

"Luck," said Clem,
"all ours has been bad!
Would you look around for
the brother I had?"

Blue quickly searched and found something odd,
It appeared that Toby was now dragging Clod!

"Let go and I'll leave, my tail has gone numb!
To come to this valley we must have been dumb."

Moaning and groaning, Clod finally sighed,
"Losing use of one's tail is just not dignified."

Blue arrived on the scene holding Clem in his grasp,
And he said, "Looks like Clod is on his last gasp!

Toby let go, you have done quite a job.
All they have left is a moan and a sob!"

Back to the Northland Blue flew with these two
And he flew very fast because frankly - P.U.!

Ole Clem was still ripe from the blast from Laverne
And he need not explain the lessons they'd learned.

Chapter 3

In the valley the gang was having some fun.
After hiding and being still, they needed to run.
They jumped and they laughed and bragged on the three
Who together had stopped the coyotes' hunting spree.

Finally someone noticed, I think it was Laverne,
That Toby's shell now had colors; was this a concern?

When Sammy and Pete spotted Toby's back,
Pete said, "I see some red and some blue and some black!"
Sammy asked, "Is that orange or maybe its pink?"
And he looked at Pete and gave him a wink.

Then everyone started trying to tell -
How many colors were on Toby's shell?
Someone said four and another said five
And they started to laugh...sakes alive!

Hal the Owl pointed out, "When all the colors blend,
I think he'll be purple! Yes, purple's the trend."

When Hal made a point they would usually agree.
Pete claimed, "You're right Hal, he looks purple to me!"

Toby dropped his head down very low.
His feelings were hurt and he wanted to go.

So he started walking away from the crowd,
Feeling ashamed when he should have felt proud.

Blue Eagle arrived just in time to see
What was happening to his old friend Toby.

"Blue, tell me please, what am I to do?
They're laughing at me here
and the turtles will too."

"Toby my friend,
I know that you feel sad,

But they didn't mean
to do anything bad."

"Importance and stature are noted by purple,
Therefore, it is fitting, to declare you a TURPLE!"

Toby hesitated and thought for a while,
Then raised his head high, thought, 'Now I've got style!'

He had an answer for his kin and the crowd;
There was no reason he shouldn't feel proud!

Then Hal the Owl, who was looking quiet serious,
Said, "This is something that I think is mysterious;

Toby has become a one of a kind -
There is no other Turple that you'll ever find!"

Then the celebration really got under way,
Laughing with each other at the events of the day.

Finally, Hal spoke
of some things we should learn

From what happened with
Toby, Arny, and Laverne.

"Don't pick on a friend who may seem inferior,
He may be a 'Turple' or something superior!

When you're feeling down or a little unsure,
Here's a good way to feel more secure:

It's TURPLEIZATION - just TURPLEIZE!
And know you're the best known you of your size!

Whatever the odds, there is always a chance;
You can lead the parade or join in the dance!

So don't be afraid to reach for a star,
You may be better than you think you are!

Yes, you are unique; you're one of a kind,
And there are no other 'yous' you can find!"

It's TURPLEIZATION - just TURPLEIZE!

THE END